St. Bernard's Seminary Library

N⁰

Given by————————————————————————

Room ————————————————————————

Department————————————————————————

The PEDANT
and the SHUFFLY

The Pedant and the Shuffly

by
JOHN BELLAIRS

drawings
by
Marilyn
Fitschen

THE MACMILLAN COMPANY : NEW YORK
COLLIER-MACMILLAN LIMITED : LONDON

BY THE SAME AUTHORS

St. Fidgeta & Other Parodies

Library of Congress Catalog Card Number: 68-15262

FIRST PRINTING

The Macmillan Company, New York
Collier-Macmillan Canada Ltd., Toronto, Ontario

Printed in the United States of America

To
DALE FITSCHEN
for unbelievably good editing sense,
endless suggestions, and seven years
of friendship

nce upon a time, in a forest of rotting crabapple trees and quaking aspens that were dying of Parkinson's disease, there lived a nasty magician named Snodrog the Pedant. Snodrog wore thick hornrimmed glasses and lived in a house made out of stolen bed slats. The shingles were old schoolbook covers, and the inside of the house was covered—walls, ceilings, and floors— with blackboards, noisy screechy blackboards that take hours to erase. The evil Snodrog would sit in this miserable house all day long, covered from head to foot with chalk dust, working out logical problems.

Since a road ran, for some boring reason, right past
his shack, Snodrog would wait until someone passed by,
then he would pop out and start an argument with
the unsuspecting victim. The passerby might be, say, a
cookie cutter, and would usually know little or nothing
about the Art of Logic. Snodrog would slowly, insidi-
ously, draw the poor person into a logical thicket, until
the victim was nodding rhythmically and Snodrog was
writing and erasing and rewriting madly on his little
portable blackboard.

At some point in the dialectical process, Snodrog would turn with a ghastly grin that looked like the ragged hole in the top of a badly opened beer can, and he would say:

"Well, if A, therefore B."

"Right."

"And if B, then certainly C."

"Right."

"Then," (here Snodrog's voice would begin to rise in pitch) "if C, why in the name of Heaven not *D????*"

"No reason why not." Here the victim usually smiled blandly.

"WELL THEN, I don't suppose you'd have any
half-witted foolish dopey oafish objection to the
inescapable conclusion that D implies E, would you??"
　　"None at all."

At this point Snodrog's voice would get very snarky
and mysterious, and he rubbed his hands together
so hard that they burned like anything.

"W-e-e-l-l the-e-n, I would imagine that even you,
with your chocolate pudding brain, could not fail to
see that E, when considered in the light of
   a.) The angle of the solar ecliptic,
   b.) Your shoe size—15 Triple E,
   c.) The fact that Jupiter, Saturn, and Topaz Minor
       are in trine, terce, bi-sextile, and yearly returns
       amounting to over six hundred million dollars,
   d.) The number of Americans killed in highway
       accidents,
   E, as I say, in the light, as it were, of all these,
proves that YOU DON'T EXIST!!!"

At this point the victim would give a little cry that usually sounded like air escaping from a leaky valve on an automobile tire. And then he would vanish with a pop, leaving behind nothing but the faint odor of foot powder. Some of Snodrog's victims, those with unusually strong wills, or those who were not entirely convinced by his

arguments, did not entirely vanish. But a more horrid fate awaited them, for they became his slaves, and were called the Flimsies.

The Flimsies usually took the shape of old linen napkins, stained with gravy and cranberry juice.

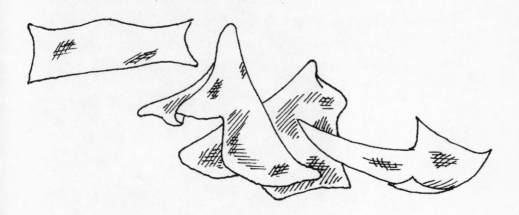

On nights when the moon was a lost pale pizza floating above the quivering treetops, midnight travelers in the forest would see the Flimsies floating by, like giant spotted butterflies on unspeakable errands. These ghostly creatures would often slip into open windows at night and try to smother sleeping people. Many a villager would wake suddenly in the purple velour darkness, his nostrils full of the odor of brown gravy and cranberries, and know that a Flimsy had gotten in.

15

Snodrog and his evil works flourished for many disgusting years, and most travelers who ventured into the Flapping Forest (as it was known) were not seen again. But one day, when the sun was like a milk bottle cap that has unaccountably gotten covered with tinfoil, a kindly old sorcerer named Sir Bertram Crabtree-Gore (Esq.) wandered into the haunted wood. He listened to the fizzing of the bees and the gentle rasping of the sapsuckers, and watched the honeyed sunlight as it dripped from innumerable palsied branches. Eventually, wearied by a day of walking, he sat down in the shade

of a crabapple tree which grew by the side of a tiny
turgid stream that seemed to be saying "uggle-guggle"
as it teased the fudgy banks and caressed the rocklike
boulders which lay in its path. Sir Bertram contemplated

18

the crabapple tree, and regretted its rottenness, for this
tree was the chief symbol on his coat of arms. He
carried a copy of his pedigree around with him, and as
he pulled it out of his carpetbag he saw the words:

19

For arms he wears a
Crabapple Tree displayed
and fructant on a field of Gore
counterfessed with Grume—the
roots of the tree clutchant, grasp a
toad, couchant, vert, who mumbles
an armed leg d'or.

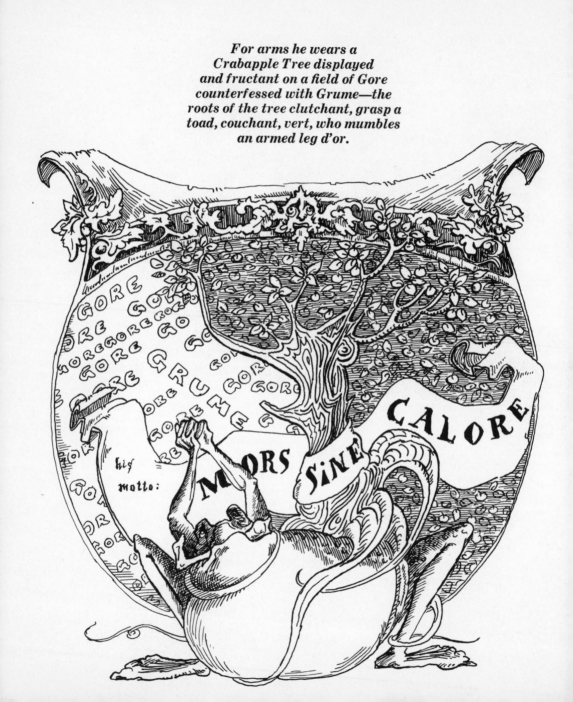

This curious escutcheon dated from the siege of Grisly Grange in 982, when Sir Bertram's ancestor Crankforth had to defend the castle with twelve men and a cellarful of crabapple preserves that his grandmother had put up. The resourceful Crankforth heated the preserves and flung the boiling sludge from catapults into the faces of the besiegers. A giant toad, attracted by the smell of the jam, came out of a nearby forest and gobbled up the tasty army.

Sir Bertram read the tale of the siege often, because it gave him strength to go on, and he read it now, sitting under his ancestral tree. He had just begun to read it for the fourth time when a voice behind him— an irritating nail-file voice—said:

"Have you ever thought that you might not exist?"

Sir Bertram answered without turning around. "Yes, I *have* thought so, but when I do, I throw myself down stairwells till the feeling goes away."

It was Snodrog, of course, all done up in his best
wizard outfit, a mauve plush affair covered with moons
and stars and square root signs. About him floated a
cloud of chalk dust.

"A witty reply," said Snodrog nastily, "but basically a shallow one. If, on the other hand, you would like to prove yourself something other than a bubbleheaded tiddly, I will argue with you."

"Oh very well," said Sir Bertram, as he did up the snaps on his carpetbag. "But I must have a day or so to think. Existence is such an important matter. Essential, actually. Why don't you go trisect a doughnut till I'm ready?"

Snodrog laughed, but his laughter was like lead washers being dropped down a storm sewer grate.

"You fool! Do you think my head is filled with kapok? Do you think you can just toddle away?" Now his voice was ominous, like soapy water drizzling from an overflowing bathtub. He raised his scraggy arms and roared:

"Flimsies! Attend me! Diaphanous sprites of the upper air, arise from putrid bog and mushy fen! Slither through quackgrass and prickly pear! Arise!"

At this a rubbery black cloud appeared overhead, sparkling with fake neon lightning. And then, to the tinny sound of unseen mandolins, the Flimsies came flitting through the wood.

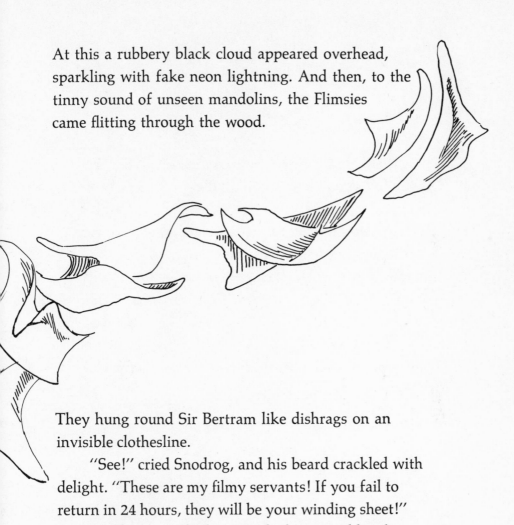

They hung round Sir Bertram like dishrags on an invisible clothesline.

"See!" cried Snodrog, and his beard crackled with delight. "These are my filmy servants! If you fail to return in 24 hours, they will be your winding sheet!"

Snodrog vanished in a peal of maniacal laughter, which is impressive if you have not seen it done before.

"Well," said Sir Bertram to the expectant Flimsies, "if you folks don't mind I think I'll go visit some friends of mine."

The Flimsies (after hurried consultation) nodded, but whether they nodded yes or no few could say. At any rate, they faded imperceptibly into the forest, and soon Sir Bertram was clumping along on a road that wound over lumpy hill and pocky dale like a strand of yellow taffy. Eventually he came to the Hagway, a road that seemed much longer than it was because it wound

through country vaguely reminiscent of northern Indiana.
Sir Bertram had been on the Hagway before, and now he
set out on the grueling journey, walking with his eyes
closed and trying to remember who had invented
logarithm tables.

It might be supposed that Sir Bertram, using this
method, would eventually stray off the road. This was,
in fact, what happened, and he was some time in
climbing out of a muddy roadside culvert. Finally, though,
around midnight, he saw a crag rising authoritatively
out of the cornfields. Atop it stood Charnel House, a
crumbling fortress which hung perilously out

32

over the abyss below and occasionally dropped pieces
of itself into the ravine. One light was burning
in the great central tower of the hall, and out of the
half-opened casement window roaring organ music
trickled. Sir Bertram immediately recognized the piece
as Buxtehude's Festival Fanfare for organ, tympani,
and tuned bass cannon.

Soon he stood under the toothless but frowning portico, and he pulled the bellrope with just enough force to break the rotting beam that supported the rusty carillon. The bells fell into unimaginable gulfs beneath the castle, and soon the door was opened by a short man in a shedding mohair ulster.

"Good evening," said Sir Bertram, deferentially, "I wonder if—"

"When Muriel Brainerd became mistress of

34

Shagcroft Manor, she little thought that she would be fighting for her life in its smelly basements."

"Hah?"

The man looked irritated. "I *said*, when Edna Clusterdug divorced Miles Gunderson to marry Alastair Waycress, she little thought that the curse of Deadfall Abbey would have her tearing her hair out on its distintegrating battlements."

"That's what I thought you said," muttered Sir Bertram. "May I come in?"

"I suppose so. Would you like a glass of bayberry wine?"

Sir Bertram followed the man into the kitchen, where the two of them put away enough bayberry wine to turn most people into Xmas candles. With an effort, Sir Bertram broke the layer of paraffin that had begun to coat his tongue, and spoke:

"Where can I get a Shuffly?"

"A Shuffly *what?*" screamed the man, who now began to roll about on the uneven tile floor.

"Please!" said Sir Bertram in a hurt tone. "I am threatened with nonexistence!"

"So are we all, from time to time," said the man, burping, and he fell asleep.

When the little man awoke, he found himself alone in the bottle-strewn kitchen, but from the tower came organ music. Tedious organ music. Sir Bertram was playing Telemann's 400 Variations on the Equilateral

Triangle, originally scored for cembalo, glass beads, and augmented ratchet.

The man raced up the tower steps, but the door to the organ room was locked.

"Come out!" screamed the man. "That is the worst deedle music I ever heard!"

"And I've got 386 variations to go," said Sir Bertram. "Where did you *ever* find a ratchet stop?"

"All right!" shrieked the man, as he began to claw

little grooves in the door. "There's a Shuffly three miles down the road in a swamp. Tell him Bozzard Craynepool sent you."

"Why should I tell him that?" asked Sir Bertram, as he opened the door.

"It's as good a name as any," said the little man. "And if you told him *I* sent you he'd probably bite your head off."

So it came to pass that, on the very next day, when twilight was beginning to seep out of the corners of the landscape, Sir Bertram was seen heading back toward the Flapping Forest. Folks could not tell for sure, but to many it looked as if he was being followed by a haystack. Now when the kindly old man and his mysterious

companion got to Snodrog's house, they found the vile logician hissing and frothing in anticipation. He had washed all his blackboards, and had practiced up by browbeating flowers and outwitting badgers; now he sat outside in a dirty striped lawn chair, next to a huge blackboard that was lit by a piece of rotting wood.

"Well," rasped Snodrog in his crankiest tone, "you

took long enough. And where did you get the portable slag heap?"

"He is no slag heap," said Sir Bertram. "He is a Shuffly, or *Scuffulans Hirsutus;* they live in fens and eat Mayflies, bulrush hearts, and linen napkins. You should have seen the one he gobbled back on the road there."

"He ate a FLIMSY!!" screamed Snodrog. An odor of chaos, like the smell of burning trash, filled the air. Long strands of linen, like tattered banners, fluttered from the Shuffly's mouth. "All right, Shuffly," gritted Snodrog. "Justify your existence. Proposition A might be phrased thus . . ." He paused and turned to Sir Bertram. "Can this overstuffed beer barrel think?"

"If you mean the Shuffly, yes, he can think," said
Bertram, lighting a rum-soaked cigar. "But I couldn't
tell you what he is thinking about at this moment."

45

"Wanna play," said the Shuffly.

"What?" muttered Snodrog, and his eyes narrowed, so that he appeared to be peering out of two flabby mailbox slots. "Proposition A, when considered in the light of certain geophysical peculiarities, leads to—"

"WANNA PLAY!" said the Shuffly, louder.

The Shuffly, lurching forward on feet clad in brown bathroom slippers, grabbed the startled Snodrog and rolled him into a ball.

"Bouncy, bouncy, bounce," said the Shuffly, as he dribbled the wizard on the footpath. Snodrog raged,

as well as he was able to, but the
Shuffly threw him over the house and
ran to the other side to catch him.
When the Shuffly got there, Snodrog
had unrolled himself and was standing
there glowering, his forehead creased
with the lines of legal trickery.

49

"Now, you shaggy hill of
loutishness," he snarled, "hear my
dread voice and tremble like the trees!
Your oversized tomb is gaping for
you!" Snodrog's eyes rolled upward
with an audible click, and he began to
chant in a voice full of vibrato:

Per ignoratio elenchi,
Per argumentum ad hominem,
Post hoc ergo propter hoc,
Barbara celarent Darii ferioque,
By the Square of Opposition, Guardian of the
Undistributed Middle,
And the Sevenfold Veil of Sophistry,
APPEAR!

Suddenly the air got colder, and a black cloud appeared—the black cloud that you saw before, since Snodrog was, at bottom, a cheapskate. Only this time the cloud looked like an overdone hamburger, and it hovered low over the Shuffly's head. A faint whirring began, and it rose till the noise was like that of a badly adjusted metal lathe. From the cloud roared a blizzard of Irrelevant Facts, and it swirled around the inert creature till he looked like a spiny snowball. Then Snodrog's devious machine spread under the Shuffly's unsuspecting feet a glistening patina of Generalizations, and the immobilized hulk slid down the hill into the valley below, ricocheting off trees with a sound like wet sponges being slapped on kitchen sinks.

Snodrog turned to Sir Bertram and sneered, and his sneer was like the high C of a bamboo calliope:

"Well? Who's next?"

Sir Bertram went on drawing pictures of the Patriarch of Alexandria on Snodrog's outdoor blackboard. After a measured pause, he spoke:

"I think he is next."

"He? Who's he?"

Snodrog felt the delicate touch of viny tendrils on
his shoulder. "Fun!" said the Shuffly, and he grabbed
the wizard by the beard and whirled him round and
round. When the Shuffly let go, centrifugal force carried

Snodrog in the direction of his own house, where his
flying body easily broke the cheap isinglass window and
came to rest in a bowl containing batter for some
eggless milkless spiceless cake he was making.

When Snodrog eventually emerged from the house, he was so angry that the batter which evenly coated his horny frame was turning to a rich golden brown. He brushed aside a dollop of goo that hung before his eyes and lifted his caky arms to the heavens.

"Flimsies! Take this mobile tumor and hurl him into the deepest most labyrinthine bog that festers on the surface of the Earth!"

There arose a sound like 10,000 bouzoukis, and from the four known points of the compass Flimsies came rustling, turning the night sky into a gravy-stained wonder of whiteness. The Flimsies wrapped themselves about the Shuffly, and the Great Flimsy, who was the size of a bedsheet or a fifty million lire note, turned into a balloon which Snodrog filled from a tank marked "Metaphysical Speculations." Borne upward by thoughts beyond his reach, the Shuffly floated over the forest till his dark bulk was no more than a muddy asterisk against the moon.

"Well? *Well?* WELL?" fluted Snodrog. His teeth made a sound like a 1916 Underwood.

"Wait a couple of minutes," said Sir Bertram, as an inscrutable smile crept down his face.

And so they waited. After several minutes had slithered by unnoticed, they saw a misshapen shadow blotching the sky. The spectral shape grew, and it soon presented (to the trained eye) the outline of a 1912 Haynes-Atkinson Structureless Inflatable Biplane, which the Shuffly had nimbly fashioned from the now docile Flimsies. "Rat-tat-tat," said the Shuffly, as he buzzed the house, prior to crash-landing in Snodrog's leek garden.

As the Shuffly crawled out of the tattered linen wreckage, Snodrog once again summoned the Cloud of Unknowing, as it was called; wearily it dragged its latex bulk over the treetops, like a ruptured blimp or an overused literary device. When it arrived it spewed at the Shuffly False Conclusions and Unproved Propositions, which danced on the creature's furry bulk in green gouts of St. Elmo's fire. Incongruencies and Hasty Assumptions leaped at the Shuffly in sheets of red lightning, and a crackly victrola voice began reciting

the First Catilinian Oration. While the great creature stood dazed, Snodrog raced into the house and came out with a cardboard box labeled "Rhetorical Ornaments." These proved to be long strands of tinsel and colored popcorn, which Snodrog wrapped around and around the inert body of the Shuffly.

When the crafty logomancer had finished his work, he stepped back to consider his tinsel-snared prisoner. He was about to order the Cloud of Unknowing to

descend and obliterate the Shuffly, when he noticed that one of the creature's eyes was blinking like a railroad signal. Snodrog came closer and poked the Shuffly in the stomach with a piece of chalk.

"Are you winking at me, you miserable lump?" he rasped.

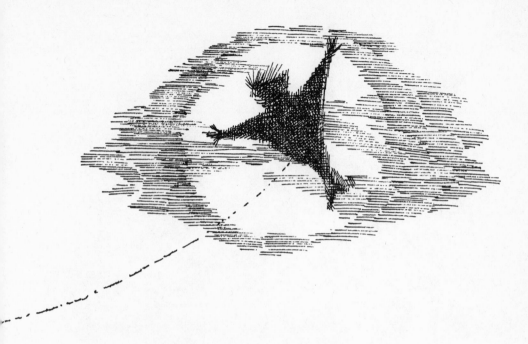

"You're cute," said the Shuffly, and he drop-kicked
the wizard into a Logical Cleft Stick that was standing
in the back yard. Then the Shuffly turned Snodrog
into a kite and flew him on a string of popcorn. After
a few hours, when the wind dropped, the wizard dropped
too, through many twitching aspen branches, and
landed at the feet of Sir Bertram, who was throwing
erasers in the air and batting them with the
blackboard.

"Why are you doing that?" panted Snodrog. His voice was round with empty speculation, but in the background was an ominous crackle, as of unseen candy bar wrappers.

"What with the little time that we have betwixt cradle and grave, what else is there to do?" said Sir Bertram, philosophically. "We toss the dusty erasers of old questions into the air and try to bat them with solid answers."

"I suppose so," said Snodrog in a statiky voice. "But why the *erasers* of old questions? Why not oranges or melons? The many-chambered tangerine of thought! How about that?"

"Your thought does not strike me as particularly chambered," said Sir Bertram, with a vaporous chuckle.

"No, I suppose not," muttered Snodrog. "But it is —how shall I say it—*calibrated*. In fact, I'd like to tell you a little secret."

"All right," said Sir Bertram. "As long as you don't slobber wetly in my ear."

"Not at all," hissed Snodrog, as he leaned closer. His breath was like a broken gas main. "The secret is that I am a *slide rule*. You've probably been wondering why my thought is so blindingly precise. Well, I am calibrated to the tiniest fraction of a degree. My thoughts have been verified by the U.S. Bureau of Standards."

Sir Bertram looked unmoved. "There are little white spaces between the lines on a slide rule. What about them?"

Snodrog looked down and began to work his belt back and forth through its buckle. "Well, let's see . . . pi times the radius squared . . . no, they're closed on Sundays from 3 to 6 . . . white spaces . . . Flimsies are white spaces! Yes, of course. *They* cover the white spaces!"

"But . . ." (Now his voice was uncertain, like a b-b rolling around in a tank.) "But . . . how did he eat the Flimsy?"

"He didn't," said Sir Bertram, calmly. "He ate a napkin. It's a sin the way people leave things around."

A fire, like the light of burning grease, was in Snodrog's dilated pupils. "Ah! That would explain it! Ah! Aaaah! AAAAAHHH!"

Before the mildly horrified eyes of Sir Bertram and the Shuffly, Snodrog began to change. His head became a glass bell-jar, his lower limbs were covered with cheap dark varnish, and he, in short, turned into a stock

ticker on a very ugly Victorian stand. Sir Bertram examined the serpentine tape that coiled from the frantically whirring machine, but all he saw at first was the number 3 followed by some random digits, which he took to be an inept attempt to work out all the places of pi. Occasionally a phrase like "Seems to indicate in the light of . . ." or "Nor can we suppose from this evidence that . . ." would apear, along with periodic statements from the Sailors and Planters Bank of Dresden, Utah.

Sir Bertram could not find any way of shutting the machine off, so he and the Shuffly went out to an all-night tavern that served bulrush beer and napkins in wine sauce. In case you are interested, all the people

that Snodrog had transformed found themselves
standing in the road outside his house the next morning.
By a curious coincidence, they were the very people
whose bed slats he had stolen, so they tore down
the house and took the blackboards home to their
children, who probably used them as sleds.

THE END